Cheryl Minnema

Johnny's Pheasant

PICTURES BY Julie Flett

Book design by Robin Mitchell Cranfield

Published by the University of Minnesota Press
111 Third Avenue South, Suite 290
Minneapolis, MN 55401-2520
http://www.upress.umn.edu

Library of Congress Cataloging-in-Publication Data
Minnema, Cheryl, author. | Flett, Julie, illustrator.
Johnny's pheasant / Cheryl Minnema ; illustrations by Julie Flett.
Minneapolis ; London : University of Minnesota Press, [2019] |
Summary: Johnny spies a pheasant, which he believes is sleeping and his
  Grandma fears is dead, but they learn they were both wrong when the
  pheasant departs, leaving behind a gift.
LCCN 2019011567 | ISBN 978-1-5179-0501-9 (hc)
Classification: LCC PZ7.M659 Joh 2019 | DDC [E]—dc23
LC record available at https://lccn.loc.gov/2019011567

Printed in Canada on acid-free paper

The University of Minnesota is an equal-opportunity
educator and employer.

25 24 23 22 21 20 19   10 9 8 7 6 5 4 3 2 1

Cheryl Minnema

Johnny's Pheasant

PICTURES BY Julie Flett

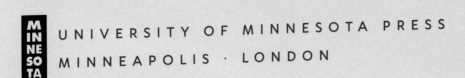
UNIVERSITY OF MINNESOTA PRESS
MINNEAPOLIS · LONDON

Johnny and Grandma were on their way home from the Grand Market with a sack of potatoes, a package of carrots, a bundle of fresh fruit, and frosted cinnamon rolls.

"Pull over, Grandma! Hurry!" said Johnny.

"What did you see?" asked Grandma.

"Come on, I'll show you," said Johnny.

Johnny led Grandma to a small feathery hump
near the ditch.

"It's a sleeping pheasant," said Johnny.

"Oh, my," said Grandma.

"Can I keep him?" asked Johnny.

Grandma gently nudged the small pheasant with her foot.

"He's still soft," said Grandma.

"Let's bring him home. I will make a nest in the yard and feed him carrots," said Johnny.

Grandma put her hand on his shoulder.

"I'm sorry, Johnny. I think he may have been hit by a car, but I can sure use his feathers for my craftwork," said Grandma.

"Silly Grandma, he's not ready for craftwork,
  he's sleeping. Let's put him in the trunk," said Johnny.

Grandma emptied a paper bag and put the pheasant
  in the trunk.

"He's still warm," said Grandma.

"Hoot! Hoot!" said Johnny.

"Hoot? Hoot?" asked Grandma.

"Yes — Hoot! Hoot!" said Johnny.

When Grandma pulled into the driveway, Johnny unbuckled his seatbelt and bolted out the door.

He leaped over each spring puddle

" Hoot! Hoot! Hoot! "

and disappeared into the house.

Johnny rushed out with a box.

"Here's his bed until I gather sticks," said Johnny.
"Can we bring him inside?"

"Okay," said Grandma. "Just for a little while."

When the pheasant was on the table and
Grandma was on the couch playing cards,
Johnny opened the door. "Okay, I'm off to get sticks."

"Hoot! Hoot!" said the pheasant.
Johnny spun around.

The pheasant shook its feathers and swooped up.

Its wings nicked the walls as it circled the living room and then landed right on top of Grandma's head.

The pheasant's tail swayed from side to side
in front of Grandma's face.

"I guess he was only knocked out," said Grandma.

"Hoot! Hoot!" said Johnny.

The pheasant sprang from Grandma's head and flew out the door.

"Hoot. Hoot. There goes the pheasant," said Johnny.

"Pheasants belong in the wild," said Grandma.

"No, he heard you talking about using him for crafts, and that's why he went away," said Johnny.

"Hoot! Hoot!" said the pheasant.

Johnny and Grandma stepped out the door
and saw the pheasant perched on the swing set.

"Hoot! Hoot!" said Johnny.

The pheasant fluttered its wings and flew away.

"Grandma! Look!" said Johnny.

A single feather zigged and zagged to Johnny's feet.

He picked it up and spread his arms.

Through the yard, Johnny zigged and zagged,

zigged and zagged, and . . .

stopped, right in front of Grandma.

He fluttered his arms down to his side and gave the feather to Grandma.

"Howah," said Grandma.

"Hoot! Hoot!" said Johnny.

Cheryl Minnema (Waabaanakwadookwe) is a member of
the Mille Lacs Band of Ojibwe. She was born in Minneapolis
and raised on the Mille Lacs Reservation by her mother,
Mille Benjamin (Zhaawanigiizhigookwe), and grandmother
Lucy Clark (Omadwebigaashiikwe). She is also the author
of *Hungry Johnny*.

Julie Flett is a Cree-Métis author, illustrator, and artist.
She has received many awards for her work, including the
American Indian Library Association Award for Best Picture
Book for *Little You* by Richard Van Camp and the Governor
General's Literary Award for Young People's Literature—
Illustrated Books for *When We Were Alone*. She has been
given the Christie Harris Illustrated Children's Literature
Award three times, and her book *Wild Berries* was selected
as a Canada's First Nation Communities Read.

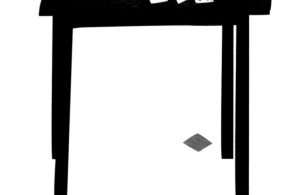

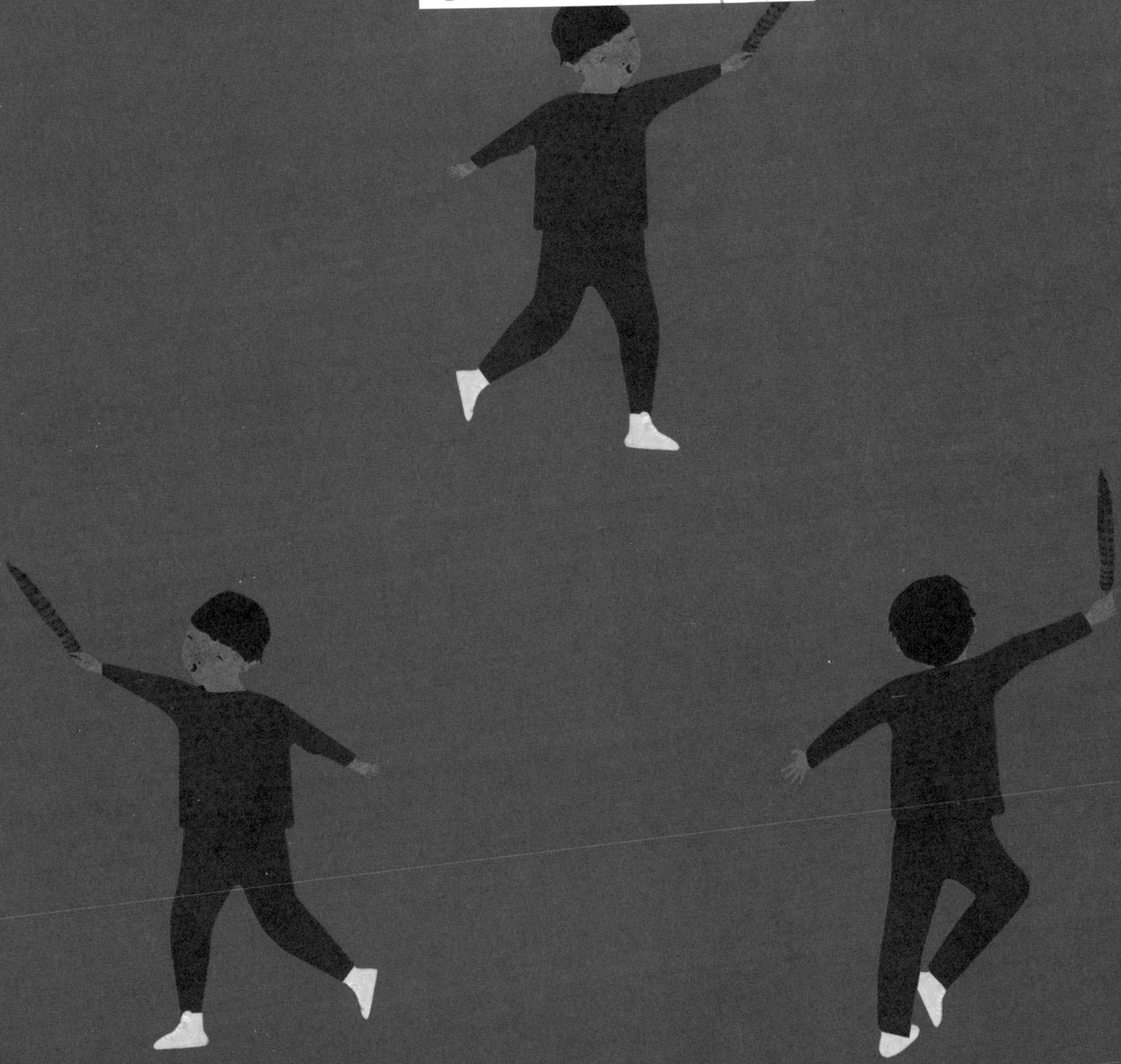